written by
Liz Garton Scanlon

illustrated by
Frann Preston-Gannon

For my cousins, my flock—L. G. S.

For Arthur, Violet, and Eleanor, with love—F. P.-G.

BEACH LANE BOOKS An imprint of Simon & Schuster Children's Publishing Division • 1230 Avenue of the Americas, New York, New York 10020 • Text copyright © 2019 by Elizabeth Garton Scanlon • Illustrations copyright © 2019 by Frann Preston-Gannon • All rights reserved, including the right of reproduction in whole or in part in any form. • BEACH LANE BOOKS is a trademark of Simon & Schuster, Inc. • For information about special discounts for bulk purchases, please contact Simon & Schuster Special Sales at 1-866-506-1949 or business@simonandschuster.com. • The Simon & Schuster Speakers Bureau can bring authors to your live event. For more information or to book an event, contact the Simon & Schuster Speakers Bureau at 1-866-248-3049 or visit our website at www.simonspeakers.com. • Book design by Lauren Rille • The text for this book was set in Artlessness. • The illustrations for this book were rendered using a mixture of both digital and hand-drawn techniques. • Manufactured in China • 0419 SCP • First Edition • 10 9 8 7 6 5 4 3 2 1 • Library of Congress Cataloging-in-Publication Data • Names: Scanlon, Elizabeth Garton, author. | Preston-Gannon, Frann, illustrator. • Title: One dark bird / Liz Garton Scanlon ; illustrated by Frann Preston-Gannon. • Description: First edition. | New York : Beach Lane Books, [2019] | Summary: A single starling is joined by hundreds more, and together they dance across the sky, finally settling into the trees. • Identifiers: LCCN 2018039906 | ISBN 9781534404434 (hardcover : alk. paper) | ISBN 9781534404441 (eBook) • Subjects: | CYAC: Stories in rhyme. | Starlings—Fiction. | Counting. • Classification: LCC PZ7.S2798 On 2019 | DDC [E]—dc23 LC record available at https://lccn.loc.gov/2018039906

DARK BIRD

Starlings are shiny, darkly feathered birds that are fast fliers and very social. Sometimes, when starlings are startled or threatened, they come together to form a murmuration—a single-seeming mass that performs coordinated, acrobatic dances in the sky. A murmuration can number in the hundreds or thousands of birds, and is quite a sight to see. . . .

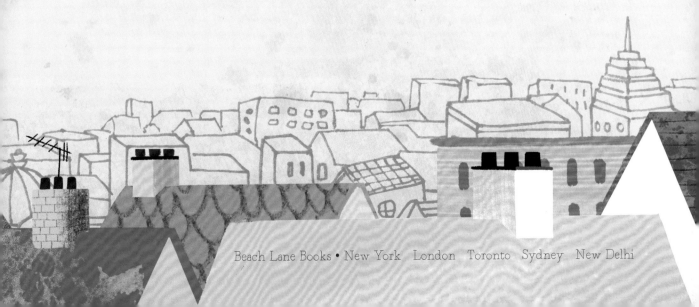

Beach Lane Books • New York London Toronto Sydney New Delhi

1

dark bird
perched way up high
a view of town
a taste of sky

2 birds more
come winging by

then 3

then 4
flights multiply

5

more swoop
around a cloud

warble, whistle
join the crowd

6 soar brightly

7 sweep

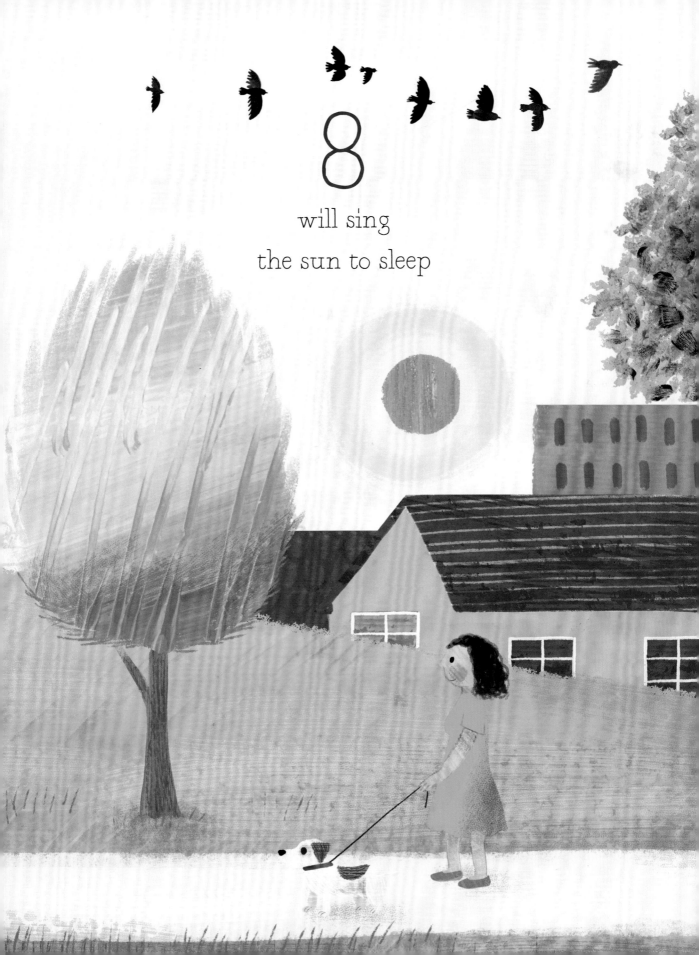

8

will sing
the sun to sleep

Then 9, then 10
from who knows where
till starling sounds
fill up the air

and there

and there

A hundred here

fine feathered friends
with sky to spare

But suddenly
they're all alert
danger's near
and flights divert!

They wheel away
from hunting hawk
single birds
become a flock

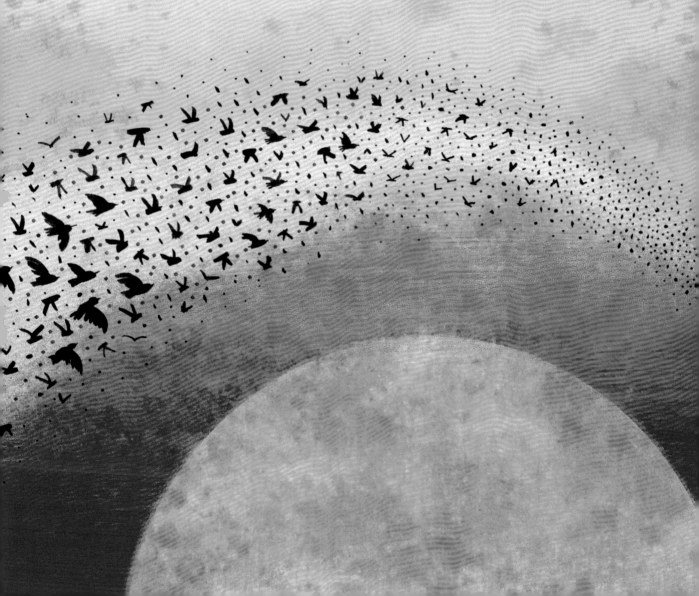

Waves like water
dark then light
from down to up
then left to right

a rush, a murmur
out turns in

a dot-to-dot

a corkscrew spin

flapping fervor
noisy clutch

they dance together
without touch

Until it's over
falls apart
each flies alone
like at the start

Hundreds here
and then, good night
they fly away
with evening's light

till just a few
float loose and free

10 birds settle
in a tree

9 land here

and 8 dive there

7 swing
in still, sweet air

6 sing softly

5 just sigh

1

last bird
perched way up high
a view of town
a taste of sky